Sabrina Sue
Loves the Sky

written and illustrated by
Priscilla Burris

New York   London   Toronto   Sydney   New Delhi

For Gina Capaldi, Kathleen Troy, and Teri Vitters

SIMON SPOTLIGHT
An imprint of Simon & Schuster Children's Publishing Division
1230 Avenue of the Americas, New York, New York 10020
This Simon Spotlight edition January 2023
Copyright © 2023 by Priscilla Burris
All rights reserved, including the right of reproduction in whole
or in part in any form.
SIMON SPOTLIGHT, READY-TO-READ, and colophon are registered
trademarks of Simon & Schuster, Inc.
For information about special discounts for bulk purchases, please contact
Simon & Schuster Special Sales at 1-866-506-1949
or business@simonandschuster.com.
Manufactured in the United States of America 1222 LAK
2 4 6 8 10 9 7 5 3 1
This book has been cataloged with the Library of Congress.
ISBN 978-1-6659-0044-7 (hc)
ISBN 978-1-6659-0043-0 (pbk)
ISBN 978-1-6659-0045-4 (ebook)

Sabrina Sue lived on a farm.
She loved being outside and
looking up at the sky.

She saw lots of birds flying around.

They looked so happy
and free!

I am a bird, Sabrina Sue thought.

I want to fly too!

She dreamed about it.

She talked about it.

Her farm friends spoke to her.

Sabrina Sue liked being silly sometimes, and brave, too.

Should she stay safe on the ground?

I really do love the sky.

She thought and thought.

She made a plan to go and
packed her bag.
She was very excited.

She hurried onto
Farmer Martha's truck.

She bounced up and down.

She flapped, and she flopped.

Sabrina Sue was ready to fly up high!

She walked under many trees.

She stomped through tall grass.

Then she looked up and saw—the sky!

Time to put on her sky gear.

Here we go—whoa!

Sabrina Sue loved the sky.

She looked for her farm
friends.

Sabrina Sue was happy to be back on the farm.
But one day she would visit the sky again!